To Mom, for sharing your love of stories with me and
providing the unwavering support, love, and encouragement to do things differently. —KK

To my family and friends, my real-life pack of markers. —LR

To my family. Who've always let me color outside the lines. —GB

IMPRINT
A part of Macmillan Publishing Group, LLC
120 Broadway, New York, NY 10271

ABOUT THIS BOOK
The art for this book was created with pencil, eraser, paper (and markers!), Photoshop, and Illustrator, using a Wacom Cintiq.
Text was set in Georgia and Avenir Next. For the title page, Timeout was used. It was edited by John Morgan and designed by Germán Blanco.
The production was supervised by Raymond Ernesto Colón, and the production editor was Dawn Ryan.

WHEN PENCIL MET THE MARKERS.Text copyright © 2020 by Germán Blanco, Karen Kilpatrick, and Luis O. Ramos, Jr. All rights reserved.
Printed in China by Toppan Leefung Printing Ltd., Dongguan City, Guangdong Province.

Library of Congress Cataloging-in-Publication Data is available.

ISBN 978-1-250-30940-2 (hardcover)

Our books may be purchased in bulk for promotional, educational, or business use. Please contact your local bookseller or
the Macmillan Corporate and Premium Sales Department at (800) 221-7945 ext. 5442 or by email at MacmillanSpecialMarkets@macmillan.com.

Imprint logo designed by Amanda Spielman

First edition, 2020

1 3 5 7 9 10 8 6 4 2

mackids.com

If you take this book without paying first,
Rest assured you will be cursed.
Every pencil you touch will snap,
And each marker you use will lose its cap.

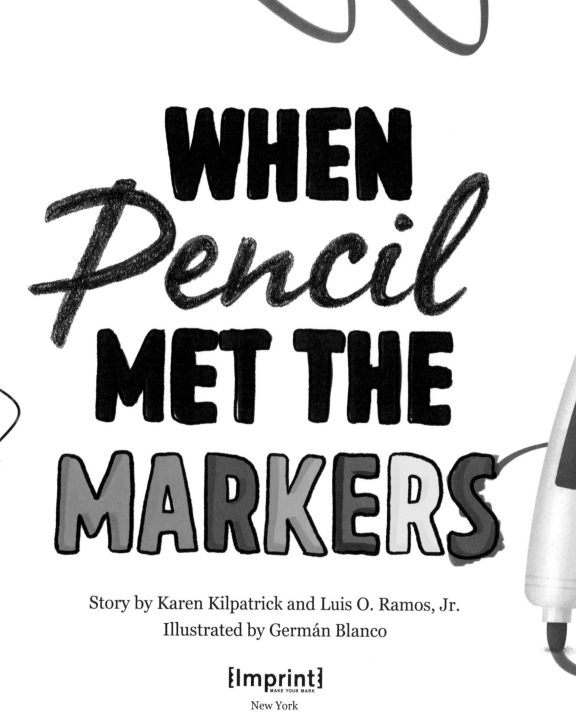

WHEN Pencil MET THE MARKERS

Story by Karen Kilpatrick and Luis O. Ramos, Jr.
Illustrated by Germán Blanco

Imprint
MAKE YOUR MARK

New York

Once, there was a pack of markers . . .

Wait for me!

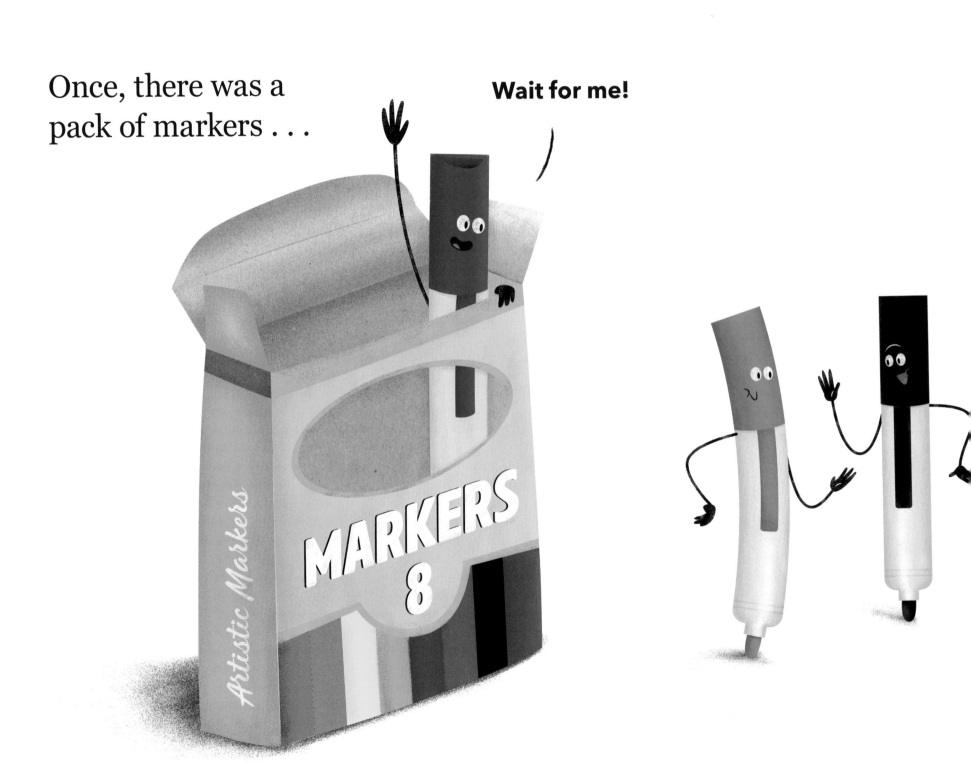

who loved to color.

And there was a
purple marker . . .

**Everyone remember,
stay inside the lines!**

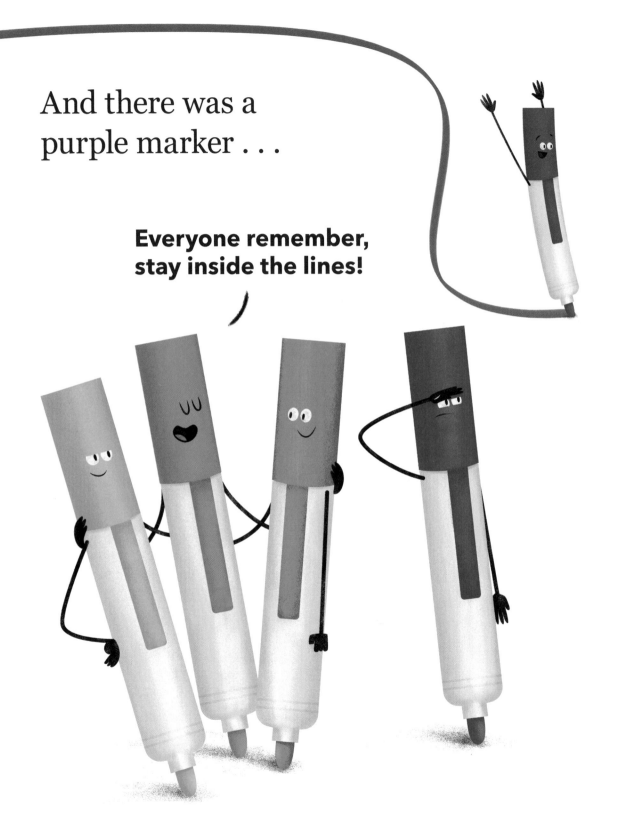

who loved to color
EVERYWHERE.

Outside the lines . . .

and all over the place.

But the other markers didn't think it was cool at all.

The rest of the
markers kept coloring
inside the lines . . .

but Purple kept coloring
outside the lines.

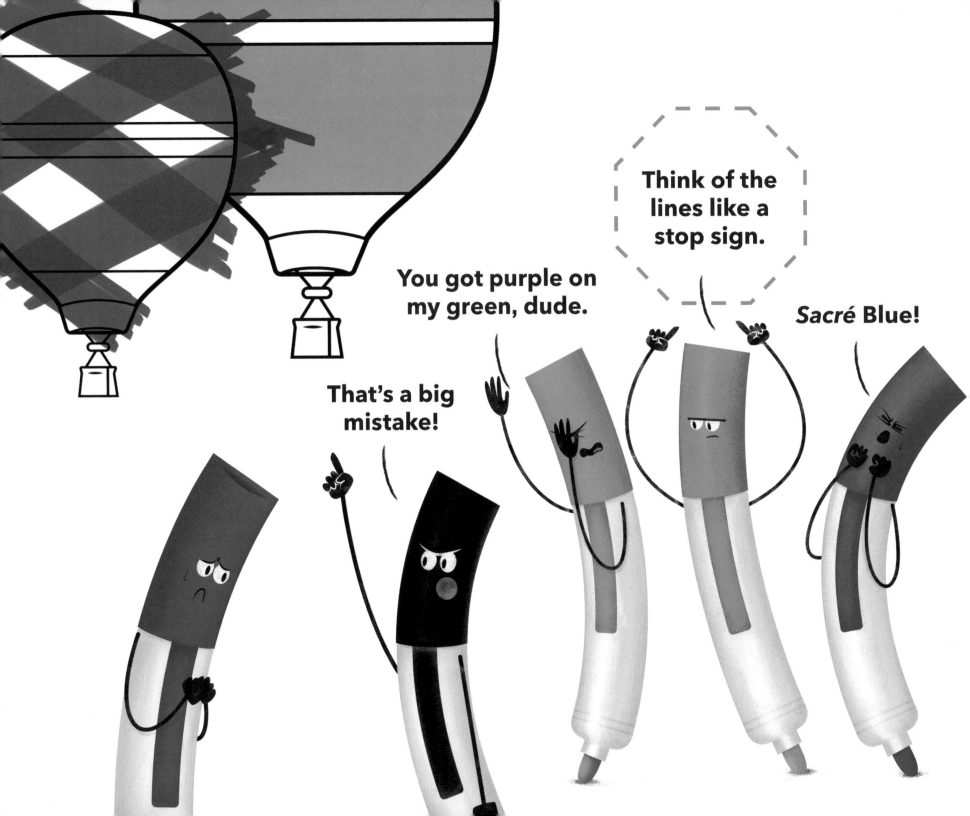

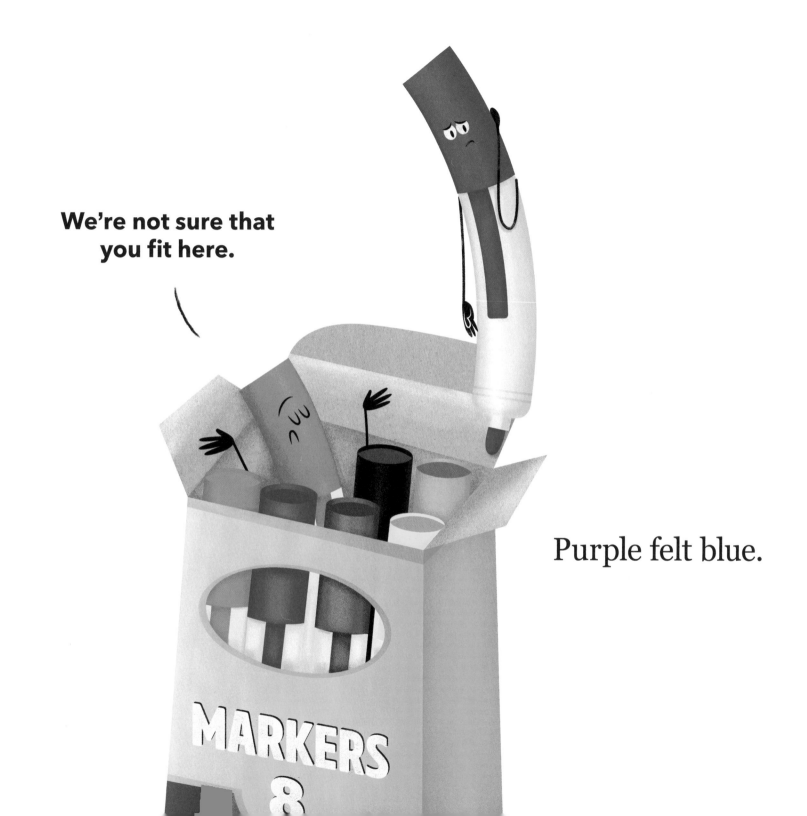

So Purple decided to
color alone.

Whatchya doin'?

But Purple wasn't alone.

But everyone knows that marker can't be erased.

I have an
idea!

Color here.

But where are the lines?

Maybe you don't need lines. Try it!

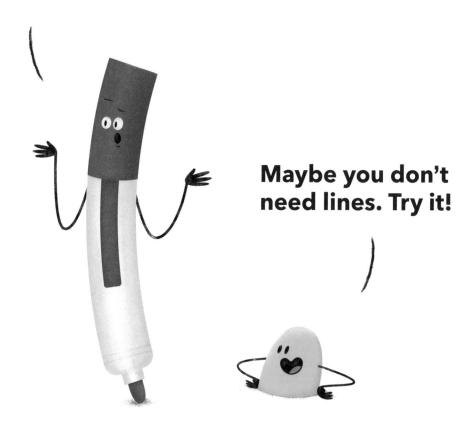

So Purple colored . . .

and Pencil drew.

Let's do another one!

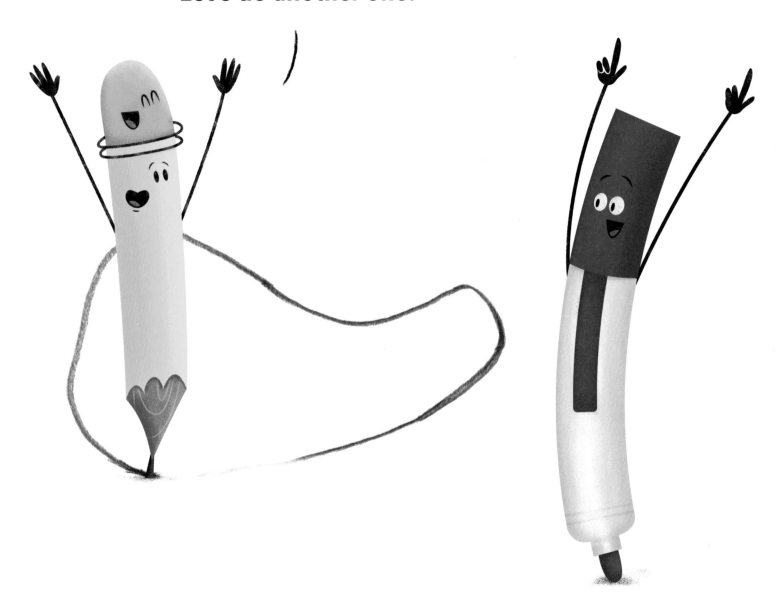

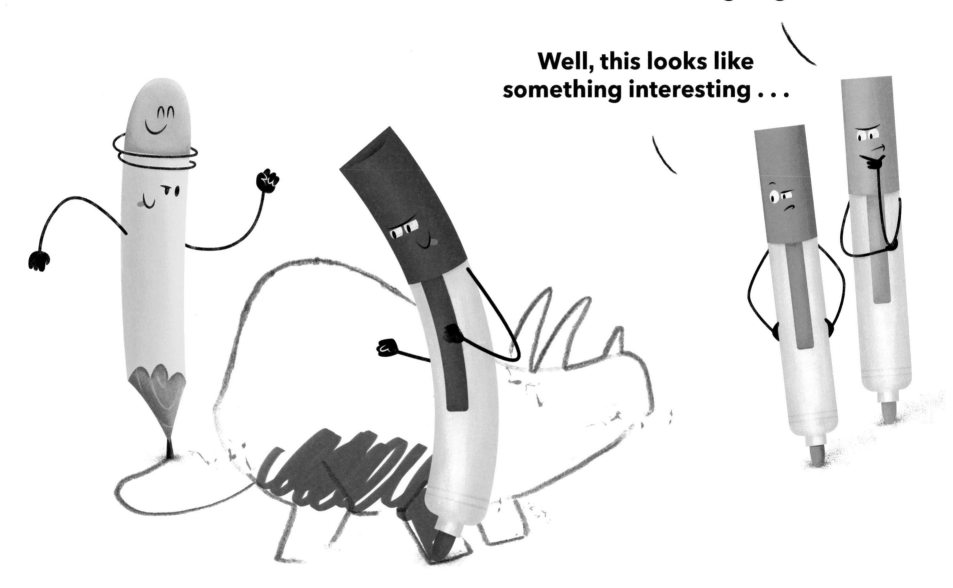

Cool, right?

And you know what?

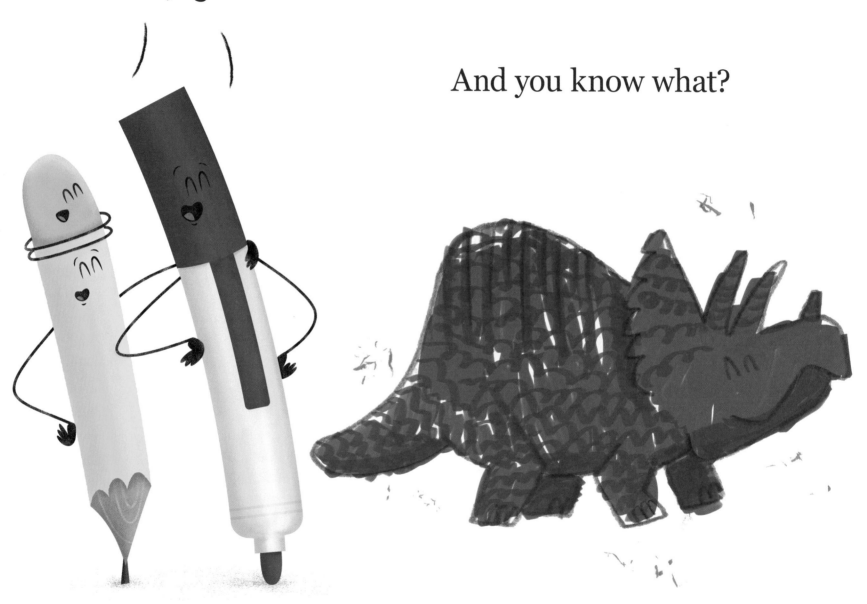

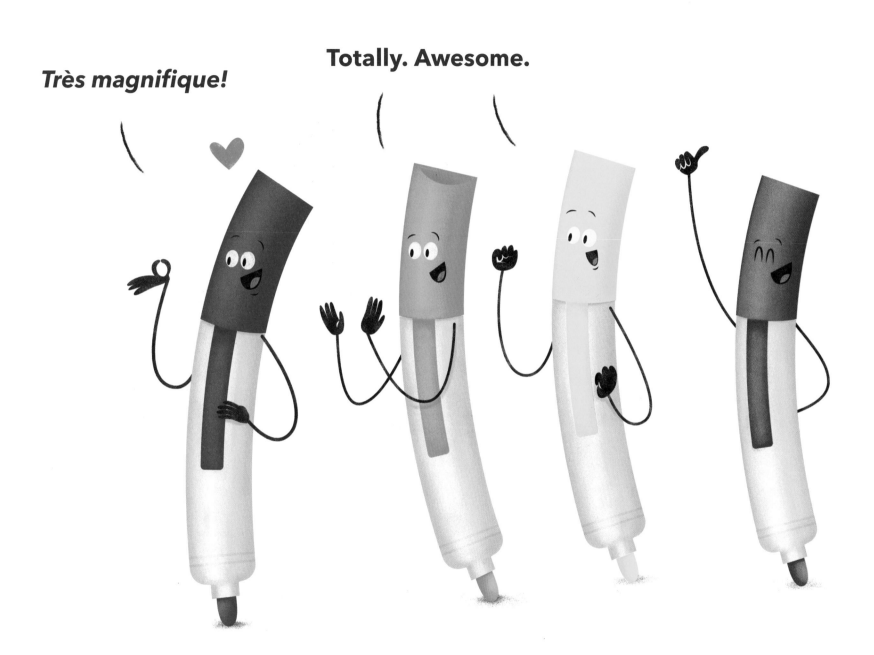

The other markers thought it was VERY cool.

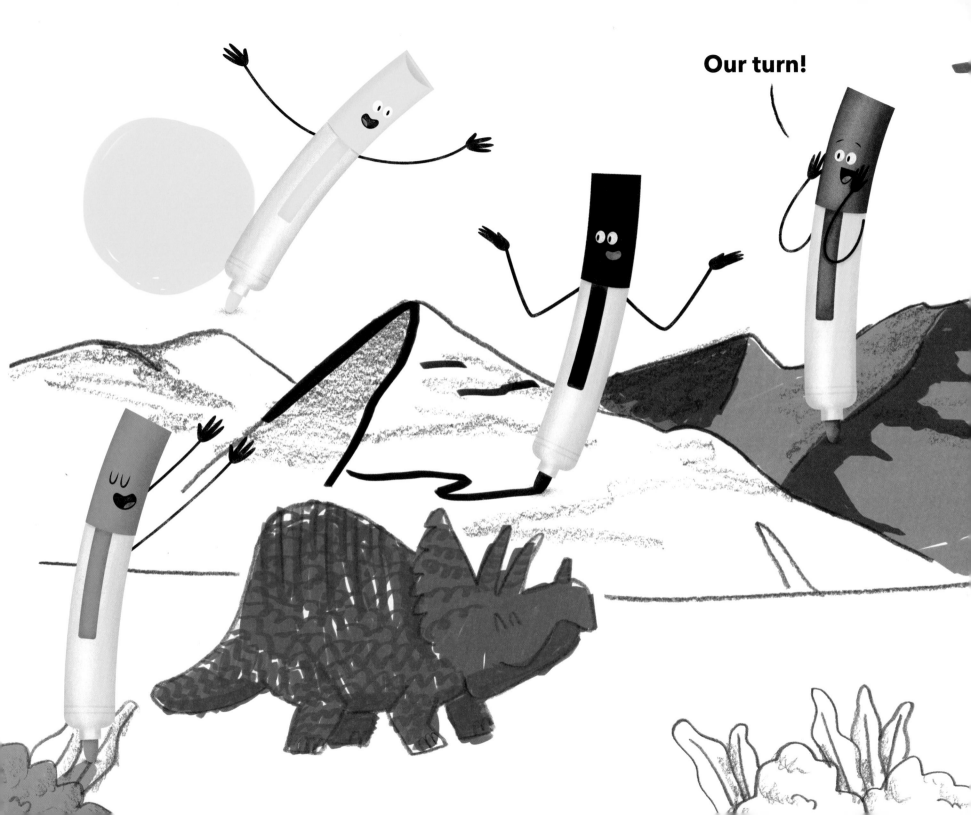

Our turn!

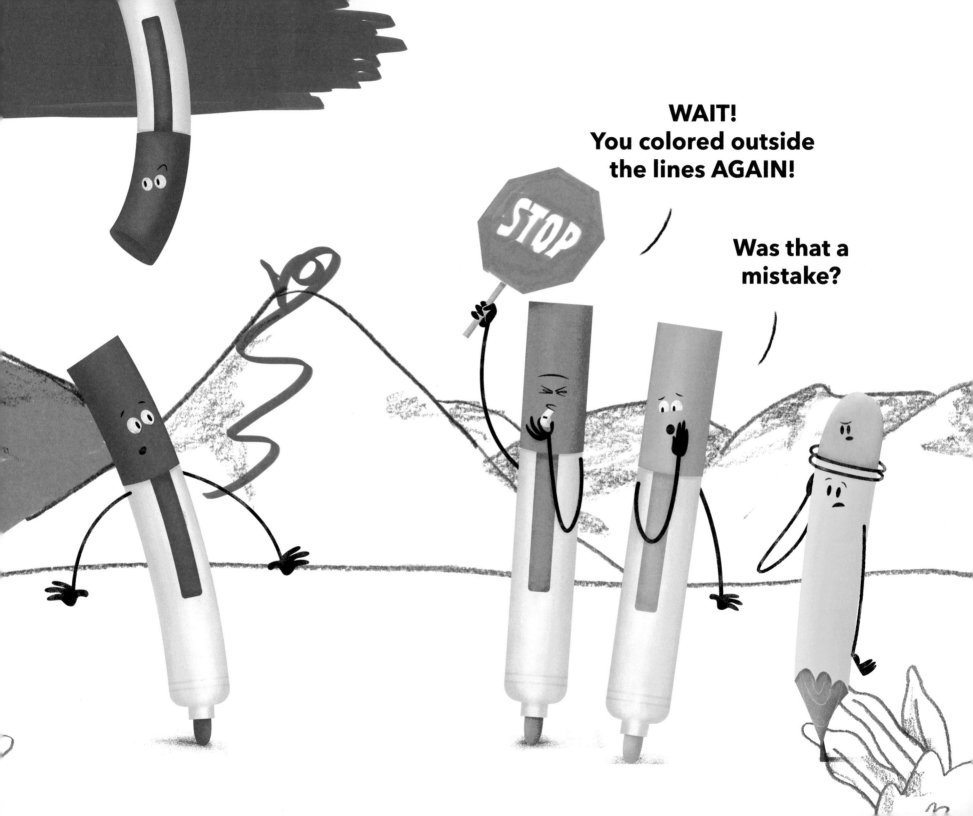

There are no mistakes,
only happy accidents!

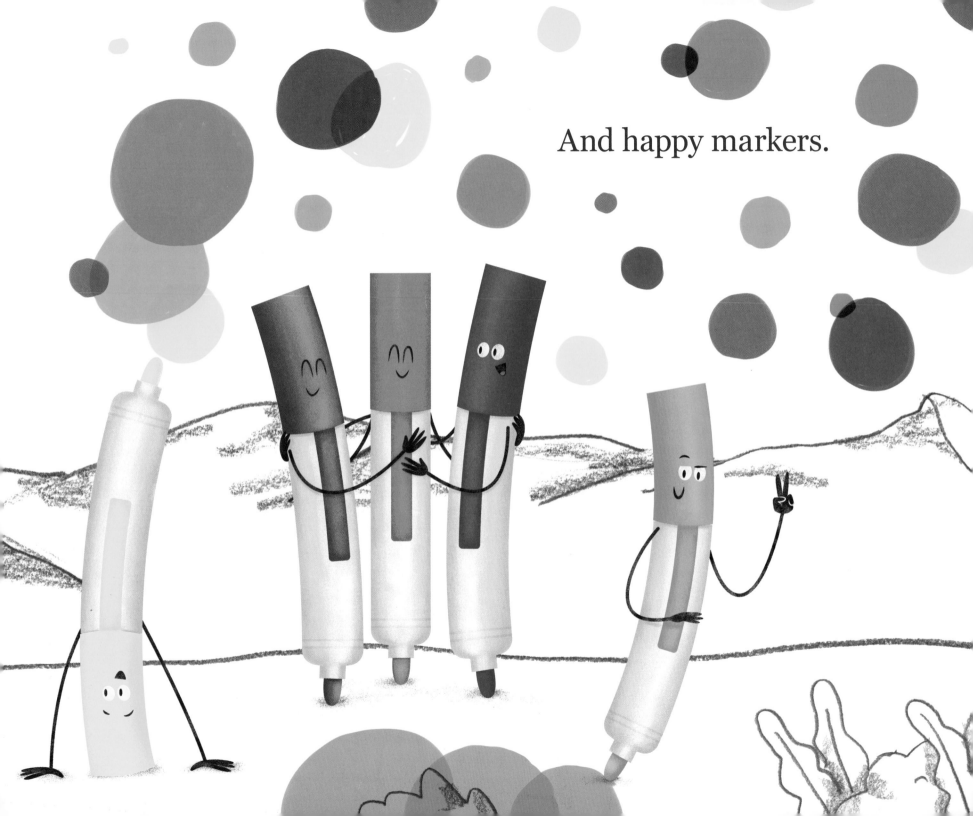

And happy markers.

So they all colored together.

And they were the
best at it!

Or were they . . . ?

The ~~X~~ End.

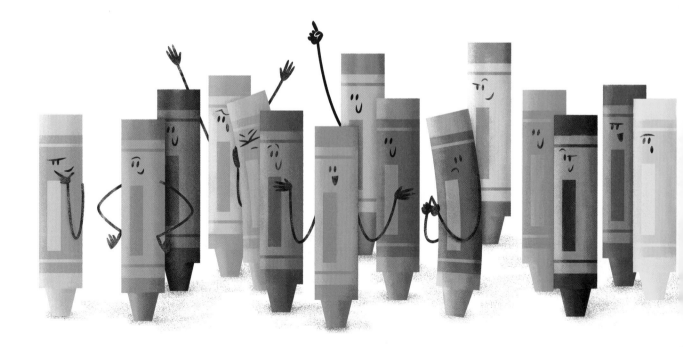